ARCHIE'S ACROBATS

WRITTEN AND ILLUSTRATED BY
CHRIS WINN

SCHOCKEN BOOKS · NEW YORK

First American edition published by Schocken Books 1984
10 9 8 7 6 5 4 3 2 1   84 85 86 87
© Chris Winn 1983   All rights reserved
Published by agreement with Victor Gollancz Ltd, London
Library of Congress Cataloging in Publication Data
Winn, Chris.
  Archie's acrobats.
  Summary: A team of acrobats who want more than
anything to be part of a real circus perform some
ingenious routines in hopes of being accepted by
Pelderfettle's World-famous Circus.
  [1. Acrobats and acrobatics—Fiction. 2. Circus—
Fiction] I. Title.
PZ7.W72973Ar 1984   [Fic]   83-10123
ISBN 0-8052-3878-6
        Printed and bound in Hong Kong by
              Mandarin Offset Ltd

Archie had a team of acrobats. They lived in
a trailer park on the edge of the town, and
every morning they practised hard.

They were beginner acrobats, and what
they wanted more than anything else in the
world was to be part of a real circus.

Then they learned
One Man Hold-me-up.

First they learned
how to do headstands
and handstands.

Then Two Man
Stand-on-the-head.

One Sunday morning, in the yard in front of the caravans,
they managed to do The Human Pyramid. Just.

"Good work," said Archie. "Now we can go into business."

"Right," said Mrs Archie. "I will be in charge of bookings."

And she nailed up a big notice. It said:

ARCHIE'S AMAZING ACROBATS

For Hire
Displays for all Occasions
Something to Suit all Tastes

And at the bottom, in bigger letters:

BALANCING ACTS OUR SPECIALITY

The first person to see the notice
was Aurion J. Pelderfettle Esq., owner of
Pelderfettle's World-famous Circus.

"Hmmm," he said, prodding the notice with a silver-topped cane. "I need a new Balancing Act. Let me see what you can do."

Archie and his acrobats did The Human Pyramid again.

"Not bad," said A.J. Pelderfettle. "Here's what I'll do. For the next week I'll come to all your bookings and watch. And if I like what I see by the end of the week, I will take you on. Goodbye."

That night, in the Chuck Wagon, Mrs Archie was boiling up prunes and custard for the acrobats.

"Pelderfettle's World-famous Circus!" sighed Archie. "We're famous!"

"Oh no you're not," said Mrs Archie. "Not yet. You will have to come up with some very special acrobatics before he takes you on. And we have a whole week of bookings to fill. Any ideas?"

For hours the acrobats thought and thought. At half past two in the morning Archie jumped up excitedly.

"I've got it!" he said. "Let me see the list of bookings Yes, yes, we will need such-and-such for this booking. And so-and-so for that. And…"

"Hold on!" said Mrs Archie. "Let me write them down and I will get them in the town in the morning."

"And finally," said Archie, "switch on the lights in the yard. We must start practising at once."

On Monday evening at seven o'clock Archie and his acrobats went to their first booking. It was for the forty professors of the Society for Egyptian Culture.

"Form ranks," said Archie to the acrobats. "Get ready. A-one, a-two, a-three—up!"

Suddenly, to the astonishment of the forty professors, there arose a mighty pyramid of acrobats!

In a corner sat Aurion J. Pelderfettle. He was taking notes.

The next booking was at nine o'clock at the Stockbroker's Ball.

"Form ranks," said Archie. "Get ready. A-one, a-two, a-three—up!"

And there, balancing on the floor of the ballroom on its handle, was a huge blue umbrella! Right at the top sat Archie.

"Taxi!" he shouted.

"Bravo!" cried the stockbrokers.

Behind a curtain stood Pelderfettle. "Shows promise," he wrote.

"Here's some Green Mountain Ointment for your
back," said Mrs Archie that night. "You were good today."

"Phew!" groaned Archie. "What a day! We'll be good
for nothing by the end of the week."

On Tuesday afternoon at three they did 'A Galleon in
Full Sail' for the Briny Harbor Yacht Club.

On Wednesday at eight they did 'Kangaroo Surprised
in the Bush' for the Australian Out-back Society at
the Embassy ballroom. This was performed upside-down.

On Thursday at nine they did 'A Seahorse Nibbling
Weeds' for the Tropical Fish Collectors' Annual Dinner
Dance.

On Friday at ten they did 'A Teapot' for Doris's Farewell Party at the Ladies' Tea and Gardening Club. What a great time that was! Even Aurion J. Pelderfettle joined in the fun.

"Commendable!" he said.

Later that night, in their caravan, Mrs Archie was rubbing Green Mountain Ointment into Archie's back.

"Ouch!" said Archie. "Not so hard Mrs A!"

"One more day to go," said Mrs Archie, "and then we will see what Mr Pelderfettle has to say."

"One more day," said Archie, exhausted, "and then we will be part of the circus."

On Saturday morning at eleven they did 'Bonzo the Brontosaurus' for the Friends of Dinosaurs Gala Biennial Open House.

At one o'clock they did
'Albert the Abominable Snowman'
for the Polar Explorers' lunch.
At two they did 'Stick Insect
Doing Back Exercises' for the
Senior Citizens Fitness Class.
At four they did 'Huge Scary
Ghost' for the Tiny Tots' Tea Party.
At six they did 'Desert
Island Castaway' for the Blue
Lagoon Cocktail Bar.

At seven they did 'Sheila the
Show-off Shark' for the
Sailors' Salty Supper.
At eight they did 'Enormous
Mouldy Swisscheese' for the
Biscuit Bakers' Banquet.
At nine they did 'Bobsy the
Twisting Pink Elephant' for
the Principals' Disco Party.
At ten they did 'Zorgle the
Thirty-legged Ploon' for the
Astronauts' Weekly Blast-off.
And at eleven—they went to bed.

It was Sunday morning. Archie and his acrobats
were so stiff they could hardly get out of their beds.
The smell of Green Mountain Ointment filled the air.
Mrs Archie was stirring porridge in the yard.

"He's coming, he's coming!" she cried suddenly. "Mr
Pelderfettle's here!"

Into the yard marched Aurion J. Pelderfettle Esq.

"Well," he said, "I'm most impressed."

"We've done it!" cried Archie. "We've done it!"

"But," said Pelderfettle, tapping his cane ominously,
"I feel your balancing acts are lacking in something.
And I can't think what it is. I'm very sorry. Maybe I'll
come back next year. Goodbye."

And he marched out of the yard.

Archie and his acrobats sank to the ground in misery and exhaustion. No circus! And after all their efforts!

"Wait Mr Pelderfettle, sir!" cried Mrs Archie, running after him. "Please wait! We have one last booking at two o'clock at the Parents' Day Bazaar. Please come, and perhaps you'll change your mind."

"Hmm," said A.J. Pelderfettle. "I'm very busy this afternoon. The circus leaves tomorrow. But I'll see what I can do."

At two o'clock Archie and his acrobats arrived at the Parents' Day Bazaar. They were very tired and very stiff.

"Good afternoon," said Miss Swivel, the principal, who was sitting in a tent on the lawn. "And what have you got for us today?"

Archie and his acrobats stumbled out to the middle of the lawn. It was very hot. Some of the acrobats were dressed in yellow, and some in green. Archie wore a big red hat, rather like a cherry.

"Right, let's make the best of it," Archie said. "Form ranks. Get ready."

"A-three."

"A-two."

"A-one."

And there on the grass, poised on its very tip was an enormous pistachio ice-cream cone made of tired, tired acrobats. Right at the top sat Archie in his red hat.

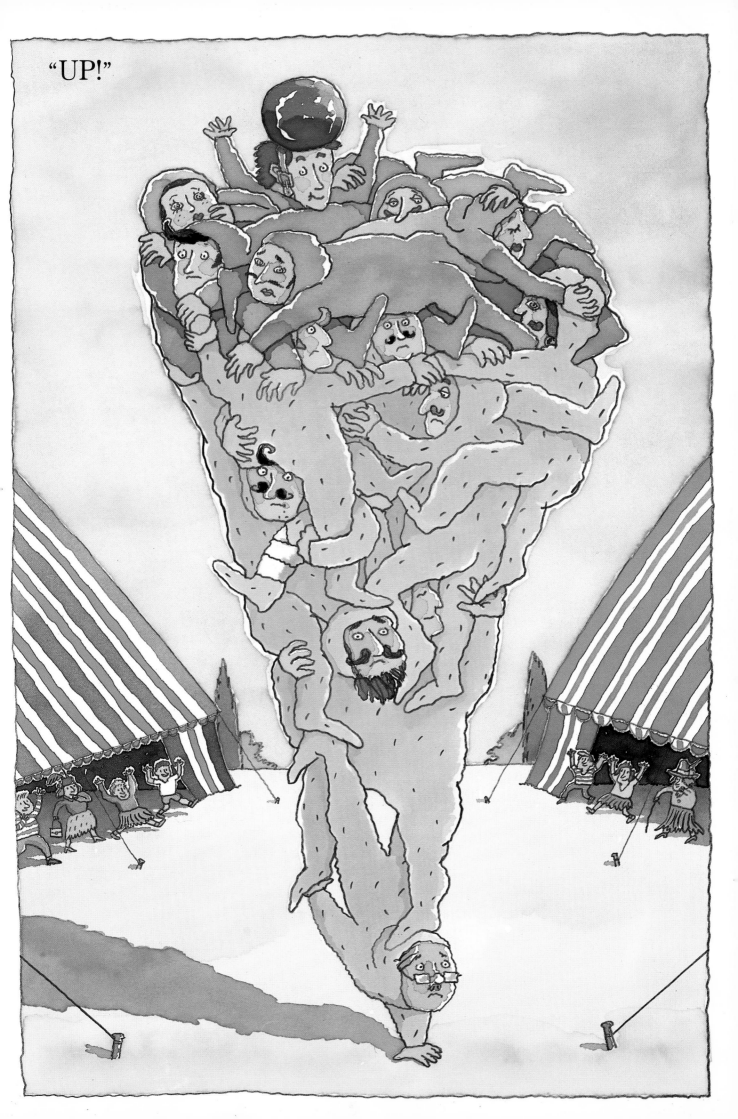

Suddenly, the ice-cream seemed to groan—and began to sway. Bravely Archie shook his red hat in the air. And as he did so, the enormous ice-cream cone swayed again, then sagged.

Then slowly,
    very slowly,
        as if it were melting, it sank.

Right on top of Miss Swivel's tent!

"Oof!" said the acrobats.

"Oh no!" said Archie miserably.

He could see Miss Swivel advancing on him with a broken tent pole. But before she could get to him, a figure strode up, his black cane glinting in the sunlight. It was Aurion J. Pelderfettle Esq.

"Magnificent!" he said. "A most moving performance. Exactly what my circus needs, and what all your other acts have lacked. A balancing act that falls over! The Greatest Unbalanced Balancing Act the World has ever Known! Here's your contract. Be at the circus tomorrow at nine."

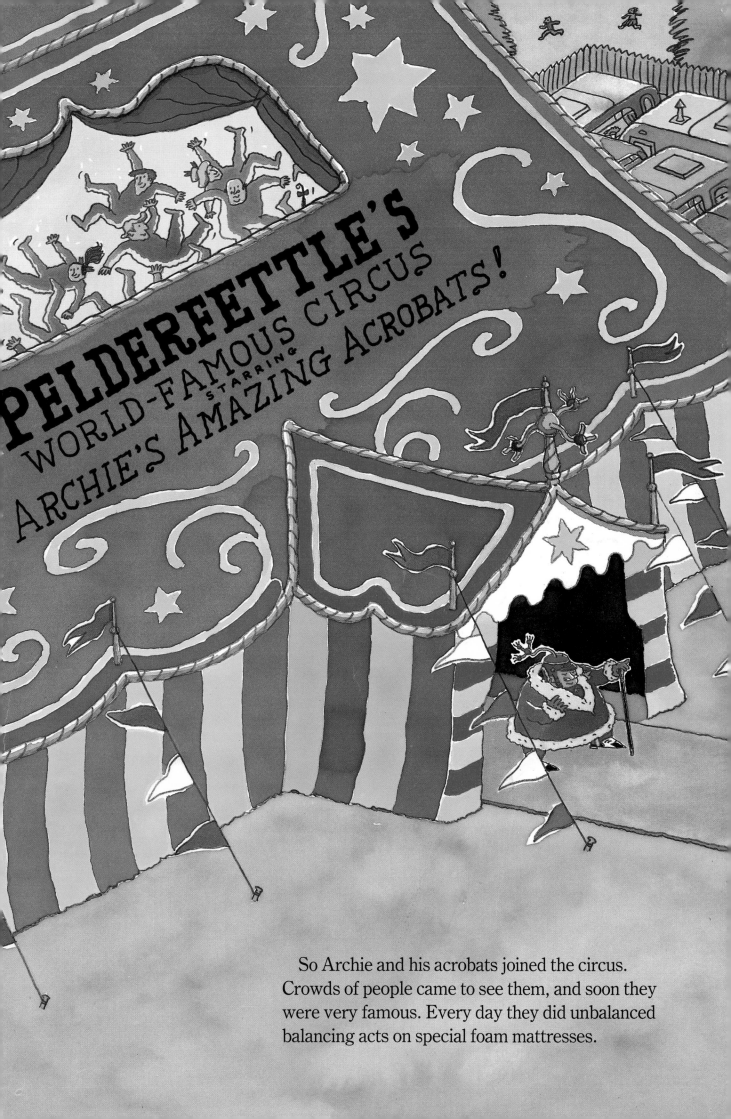

So Archie and his acrobats joined the circus. Crowds of people came to see them, and soon they were very famous. Every day they did unbalanced balancing acts on special foam mattresses.

And every night Mrs Archie rubbed
Green Mountain Ointment on them.

Juno

Foxy & Mrs Foxy

Blinko

Curlo

Archie

Atlas

Silvini